Cory Cucumber and the farmyard muddle

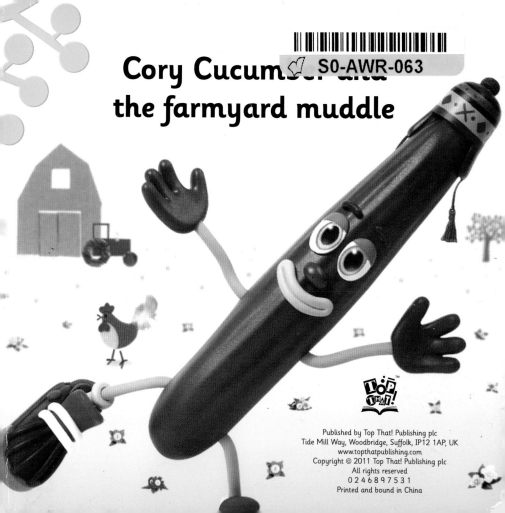

Published by Top That! Publishing plc
Tide Mill Way, Woodbridge, Suffolk, IP12 1AP, UK
www.topthatpublishing.com
Copyright © 2011 Top That! Publishing plc
All rights reserved
0 2 4 6 8 9 7 5 3 1
Printed and bound in China

What scene have the
children made today?

A busy farmyard...

One day, Cory Cucumber stepped into the children's playscene. The children had created a busy farmyard.

Cory thinks that he is the coolest Frooble and he is always showing off in front of his friends.

Cory spotted the farmer and walked over.

"Do you need any help?" Cory asked.

"Have you worked on a farm before?" asked the farmer.

"No, but working on a farm will be a piece of cake for a Frooble like me!" said Cory.

The farmer asked Cory to collect eggs from the hens, feed the pigs, milk the cow, saddle up the horse and herd the sheep into the next field.

"Ask for help if you need it," said the farmer.

"That sounds easy!" Cory replied.

Confident that he would soon complete all his tasks, Cory decided that he would collect the eggs first.

But, he walked straight past the henhouse and went to the pigpen instead.

To collect eggs from the pigs!

Cory looked under every single pig in the pen, but as you would expect, he did not find a single egg!

"I'll come back when the pigs have laid their eggs!" said Cory, leaving the hungry pigs waiting for their breakfast.

Next, Cory walked across the busy farmyard to feed the hens.

"You must be hungry," said Cory to the hens, emptying buckets of pigs' food onto the ground.

BOK, BOK, BOK! The hens took one look at the pigs' food and then went back to their henhouse.

"Oh well, I'll come back when the hens are hungry," said Cory, and he left the hens' eggs uncollected.

Next, Cory walked over to the stable where the horse was waiting.

And then Cory did the silliest thing…

He tried to milk the horse!

"These are very difficult chores!" said Cory, as the horse angrily kicked over the milk bucket. "I hope the next chore is easier!"

But, it wasn't.

Cory couldn't make the horse's saddle fit the cow, because the saddle was not meant for her!

"Being a farmer is much more difficult than I thought," said Cory.

Cory had one task left to do.
He had to herd the sheep and
move them to another field.

"How am I going to move all
these sheep?" thought Cory.
Then, he spotted Chloe Carrot.

"Chloe!" shouted Cory.
"Please will you help me
to herd these sheep
for the farmer?"

"Of course I will," said Chloe.

But Chloe whizzed into the field too quickly and startled the sheep. The sheep scattered and ran out of the field!

"Oh no! I should have asked the farmer for some help!" sobbed Cory.

Cory didn't want to tell the farmer about all his mistakes, but he knew that it was the right thing to do.

The farmer was very annoyed. But, he was also very impressed that Cory had been brave enough to tell him the truth.

So, the farmer showed Cory how to collect eggs from the hens, feed the pigs, milk the cow and saddle up the horse.

"This is much easier than before," said Cory.

With help from the farmer's dog,
Cory and the farmer even managed to
herd the sheep.

Cory felt much better, and he was happy
that he had managed to help the farmer
after all.

Now, whenever Cory doesn't know how to do something, he always asks for help first.

And that makes Cory very cool indeed.